THE MAGIC MIRROR

THE MAGIC MIRROR

Linda Moffit

Illustrated by
Ellen Drucker

DeVorss & Company
Box 550, Marina del Rey, CA 90294–0550

ISBN: 0-87516-615-6
Library of Congress Catalog Card Number: 89-50125

Printed in the United States of America

With
immense love
and
heartfelt gratitude,
I dedicate
this book to:

My very grown-up, beautiful son, Michael Moffit, who reminded me for so many years of the beauty and imagination which lies in the mind of a child.

My lovely little niece, Sonnet Anastasia Sadoski, to whom I wrote the story and whose name provides the central character, Princess Anastasia. But she is not the Anastasia of this story. Also to her beautiful mother, my sister, Althea Sadoski, who has always provided me with love and support.

My wonderful friend, Jerri McCranie, Religious Science practitioner, who first introduced me to Religious Science and who encouraged and supported this writing so lovingly.

My beautiful friend, teacher, counselor and minister who taught me the principles of Science of Mind and trusted me to apply them appropriately, the Reverend Michael R. Santo of the Tampa Bay Church of Religious Science.

L. M.

THE MAGIC MIRROR

It seemed like a pretty normal day to the people of the castle. Having been up for several hours, the good people had their work well under way. The Queen was busy with her queenly duties. The King was conducting kingly business. The upstairs servants had their cleaning pretty much done, as did the downstairs servants. The cooks in the kitchen had long since prepared and cleaned up after the morning meal and were preparing for lunch. Good smells drifted all over the castle as a result of their long hours of work.

Still, they were all aware that another part of the normal routine was only due to begin. Then it began suddenly when the chambermaid rushed headlong down the many stairs, ran down a long hall, and disappeared around a corner. The entire castle seemed to halt as everyone listened for the next sounds.

Stomp, grumble, mutter, stomp! Stomp, stomp, stomp! The Princess Anastasia came down the long stairs. As she descended, she grumbled and muttered in her anger at the chambermaid. Stomp, grumble, mutter, stomp! Stomp, mutter, grumble, stomp! And so she came down the stairs. As she arrived at the bottom, she caught a glimpse of herself in the huge mirror in the great hall. Convinced that her scowl was not nearly frightening enough, she paused to fix her face into an even deeper scowl and then proceeded to the kitchen.

As she approached the kitchen, the maids scurried out the door to the kitchen garden and busied themselves there. The cooks hurried to the farthest end of the kitchen and buried themselves in their pots and pans. The kitchen dog ran out the back door to the stables with the kitchen cat fast at his heels.

Mindless of all this haste, with a stomp, grumble, mutter, stomp! the little Princess arrived in the kitchen.

"I'm hungry!" she barked. "Bring me my oatmeal!"

The cook was already on her way with the steaming bowl. She quickly set it down and beat a fast retreat.

Greedily, the Princess gulped down the oatmeal and jumped up from the table. She stomped her way to the kitchen door. She slammed the door. She stomped her way down the path to the stables. And she did not notice as the kitchen maids kept their distance and returned to the kitchen to take up their tasks.

Stomp, stomp, stomp! Grumble, mutter, stomp! Princess Anastasia stomped her way to the stables. As she stomped, she kicked an occasional pebble. Then she grumbled and she muttered. Then she stomped and kicked another pebble. Then she muttered and she grumbled again. The kitchen dog saw her coming and quietly tucked his tail between his legs while he hid himself behind a large pile of hay. The kitchen cat, taking note of her arrival, scurried up a ladder and into a loft to watch her progress from above.

Alas, the stable boys had not seen her! In the doorway of the stables, the boys were playing a game of marbles. Three stood around the circle of marbles and two were kneeling right beside it. Spying the game and the marbles in the center, the Princess stomped her way to the center and brought her foot down hard right in the middle. The marbles scattered in every direction. Some rolled under a nearby door. Some rolled under the hay. Many were lost and never found again.

Angrily, she stood in the midst of her handiwork (or perhaps it should be called her *footwork*) and glared defiantly at the stable boys. She knew that they wouldn't dare say anything to her. She was right, too, for they quietly looked at the damage, bowed their heads, and turned to their work.

Satisfied that she had broken up the game for those no-good, lazy stable boys, Anastasia stomped her way through the stables. Annoyed that she could find no one else about the place, she stomped away from the stables.

"The Princess Nasty has gone!" shouted one of the stable boys.

At that, they all burst into laughter as they watched the Princess stomping up the stable path. Now she was muttering about those no-good stable boys. She kicked an occasional pebble. She grumbled and she muttered. She muttered and she grumbled. Then she kicked another pebble. Stomp, stomp, stomp, stomp! Grumble, mutter, stomp!

P rincess Anastasia stomped her way up the stable path
and out of the huge castle gate. The drawbridge was
down, so she stomped across the moat and made her way
to the quiet village on the other side.

The village was sprawled just outside the castle. There
were dozens of small thatched huts huddled peacefully
together in the noonday sun. Dogs lay sleeping in many
doorways, and chickens scratched in the warm earth of the
little yards. Occasionally a villager, busily about his daily
work, peeked at the Princess from the shadows of his hut.
Once in a while, a villager crossing the narrow streets would
pass hastily by Anastasia, offering a polite bow and a mum-
bled "Good day, Your Highness."

Princess Anastasia hardly even looked at the villagers. She had little to say to these people. She felt that they were very lazy, and she had no time for them at all. In the distance, she could hear the sounds of children's laughter. She tried to follow the sound for a while, but every time she got a little closer, it seemed the laughter stopped. Then she would hear it again, this time from another direction and farther away.

Tiring of the chase, Anastasia once again turned her feet toward the castle. She stomped her way across the drawbridge over the moat and through the castle gate. Now she turned in the direction of the King's gardens.

As she approached the gardens, she could see one of the gardeners bent over his work. He was planting a row of lovely pink flowers deep into the good earth. Angrily, Anastasia ran to the flowers and, following just behind the gardener, began to pull them up from where he had just planted them. Surprised and dismayed, the gardener turned toward her.

"Here!" Anastasia cried, throwing the beautiful flowers at his feet. "Plant them again! You've chosen the wrong place for them. Put them over there by the white flowers. Anyone should know that! You can be so stupid!"

The Princess spun on her heel and marched down the garden path. As she passed the huge sundial in the center of the lovely garden, she could see the time as the sun cast its shadow from high above.

It was time to visit the Queen Mother! Anastasia was allowed to visit the Queen Mother at this time every day. She hurried back toward the castle. Hurrying through the great hall, she stopped in front of the huge mirror and once again checked her frown to see that she looked properly stern for a Princess. Satisfied, she hurried up the wide staircase, turned down a long hall, and stopped at a room at the far end. She knocked quietly at the door.

The door was opened by the Queen Mother's personal lady, the fair maid Lillian. Seeing the young visitor, Lady Lillian said, "I will announce you."

She returned in just a moment to admit the little Princess.

On entering the lovely room, Princess Anastasia immediately saw her beautiful grandmother sitting gracefully in the afternoon sunlight near one of the large windows. The Princess was never quite prepared for the beauty of the Queen Mother. Her hair was soft and golden still, as it had been when she was young. It was pulled back elegantly to the top of her head and fixed there with a set of silver combs. She was dressed in a gown of satiny rose with little silver bows covering it. But what really attracted Anastasia was the Queen Mother's lovely face. It always wore a beautiful smile. She was by far the most warm and loving person the Princess had ever known.

The Queen Mother smiled her beautiful, gentle smile at Anastasia. "Good day, my child. How are you today?"

The Princess pulled up a small stool near the Queen Mother and seated herself.

"Oh, it isn't really a very nice day. I have been having a most terrible time!"

"Really, child? And how is that?"

"My chambermaid started everything off all wrong the very first thing when she brought me the wrong dress. I don't think that girl can do anything right! And the cooks are so stupid! I caught the stable boys playing when they were supposed to be working. They are such a lazy lot!"

The Queen Mother smiled gently, "So it would seem."

"I was in the village for a little while, too. *There's* another bunch of really lazy people! The King and the Queen really must take a firmer hand with them. They need to work harder. They have too much spare time!"

Nodding gently, the Queen Mother smiled her sweet smile again. "So it would seem."

"When *I* am the Queen, I will make a lot of changes. There'll be no more loafing by any of the people in the kingdom. I simply won't permit it!"

"So it would seem, so it would seem."

"The servants don't serve me well! I know they do better for the King and the Queen. I just don't understand why they would serve the King and the Queen better than they serve me. Do you understand that, Queen Mother?"

"The King and the Queen learned the lessons of service long ago."

"Learned the lessons of service?? I don't understand that. The King and the Queen have never had to serve anyone in their entire lives. That's what it means to be a King and a Queen!"

"So it would seem." Again the soft sweet smile.

"And another thing: I don't have anyone to play with, Queen Mother."

"You will have many, many friends as soon as you are ready for them."

Puzzled by this response from the Queen Mother, Anastasia decided to let it go. She really wanted to hear a story anyway. That was why she had come. And so it was not long before the Queen Mother was telling her one of her many stories of how the kingdom was when she was a child and the places she had been and the things she had done. And so the time passed until it was time to go.

Being with the Queen Mother often changed the Princess for a little while, and so it was that she forgot for a few minutes to stomp and grumble and mutter as she went down the hall and started down the stairs. But by the time she had arrived at the great hall mirror, she stopped to fix her scowl firmly in place and proceeded down another of the halls.

Nearing the door of the Queen's quarters, the Princess stuck out her chin at the lady who met her at the door.

"I wish to see the Queen!" she demanded.

She didn't know that the lady had already received her instructions from the Queen. The day was far too busy for the possible temper tantrums of the Princess.

"The Queen has left instructions not to be disturbed today."

"I wish to see the Queen!" Anastasia demanded even more loudly.

"I am sorry, but the Queen has instructed me."

"I *demand* to see the Queen *right now*!!" Anastasia was so angry that she could hardly contain herself. How dare this woman of lesser birth refuse her admission to the Queen!

There followed quite a few words between the angry little Princess and the firm, loyal lady, but the Princess could not get her way. After some time, she stomped down the hall again. Stomp, grumble, mutter, stomp!

A nastasia proceeded back to the great hall and down still another of the large hallways to the King's offices. She was still too far away to get the attention of her father as she saw him disappear around a corner with several important-looking men in elegant coats.

Disappointed that she had missed him, she paused at the door of the room they had just left. She wandered inside a bit and strolled around the chairs in which they had been seated. She sat in some of them, but they were far too big for her, so she gave up on that. Then she just wandered about the room handling the different objects placed on a table here and a table there. Bored with the big room, she was about to leave when she noticed a small door almost hidden by a large chair in the corner of the room.

Princess Anastasia walked over to the little door and gave it a tug. Surprisingly, it opened readily. She was standing at the door of a rather small room which seemed packed with just about everything. She guessed it was some kind of a storage area. There were boxes—many, many boxes—piled high all over the room. Some were draped with clothing of every color and description. There were a variety of desks and chairs and odds and ends of all kinds. It was just like the kind of room children of today might call an attic.

Intrigued, the Princess walked in and strolled among the boxes. She looked at the chairs. She looked at the desks. She admired the little things sitting on the boxes and scattered around the room.

Finally, her attention was caught by a large box sitting right in the middle of the little room. She recognized a familiar color on top of the box and walked over to get a closer look. She tugged on a piece of blue cloth and pulled it out. Yes, it was one of the gowns belonging to the Queen. Princess Anastasia had seen the Queen wearing this on the night of a great ball. It was quite lovely. It had probably been placed here because the Queen rarely wore a gown more than once.

Curious, the Princess pulled the gown over her own head. It was way too large. But Princess Anastasia was a determined little girl. She went over to the box and looked down into its contents. Inside, she saw even more beautiful gowns belonging to the Queen. She pushed this one aside and that one aside until she found one with a beautiful golden belt. She gave the belt a tug and pulled it out of the box. Then she wrapped it around her waist. She thought that was better.

Then she rolled up the long sleeves—first one sleeve and then the other. That was better.

Next, she gathered the long skirts together in her hands and lifted them off the floor. Yes, the dress seemed almost to fit her now.

Looking around the room, she made another find. Just a little way off, in another corner, there appeared to be a mirror. Princess Anastasia thought she would see how the gown looked. Making her way between the boxes, still holding a part of her long skirt up from the floor, the Princess approached the mirror. It was a small one, just a little taller than she was. It was just the right size.

The Princess stood before the mirror and surveyed the effect of the beautiful blue gown. Maybe not a perfect fit, but one could see that it was the kind of gown a Queen would wear. Anastasia very much liked the way she looked. So she pulled herself up tall, the way she felt a Queen would, and she walked in what she hoped was a queenly manner back and forth in front of the mirror.

Caught up in her fantasy, Anastasia began talking. "There'll be no more loafing, you lazy lot! Work, work, work!"

Remembering that a scowl was a very important part of her idea of how a queen should act, Anastasia remembered to deepen her scowl and looked into the mirror to catch the full effect.

"There'll be no more loafing, you lazy lot!" she shouted into the mirror.

The Princess was so surprised at what she saw that she could not believe her eyes. She scowled even more deeply and stepped closer to the mirror. She looked into the face of the girl in the mirror. There was the most beautiful smile she had ever seen! The girl in the mirror was smiling out at Anastasia with a most angel-like and gentle smile!

Anastasia tried again. She screwed her face up into the most horrible scowl she could possibly imagine and looked into the mirror. Once again, the girl in the mirror was smiling back sweetly at her. The only change was that perhaps the smile was even more beautiful and shining than before!

Anastasia was surprised. So surprised, in fact, that she jumped back and almost tripped over the long skirt she was wearing.

Now she approached the mirror slowly. She looked carefully at the image in the mirror. Here was the beautiful blue gown. Here was the shining gold belt. Here were the rolled-up sleeves and the tucked-up skirts. She carefully checked every detail in the mirror. She looked at the room in the mirror. Here was that box; there another box. She turned around and looked at the room directly. Yes, that box was just like its mirror image. Yes, another box was just like *its* mirror image.

How strange! She turned again to the mirror. Yes, there was the little Princess standing in the mirror image exactly as she was—except for that face. Princess Anastasia slowly raised her arm. The girl in the mirror did the same. She lowered her arm carefully to her side. The little girl in the mirror did the same.

Then she raised her arm quickly. So did the image in the mirror.

She lowered it quickly. So did the image in the mirror.

She turned to one side. So did the image.

She turned to the other. So did the image.

Then she tested it again. Putting on her most horrible scowl, the Princess checked again in the mirror. There still was that bright, sweet smile!

She jumped up and down. So did the image.

She tried it again. So did the image.

She turned quickly away from the mirror and spun to catch it by surprise. But still there was that beautiful, sweet smile! Angry with it all, Anastasia spun away from the mirror, walked a few steps, spun around and ran back to the mirror with another horrible scowl on her face. Still, a beautiful smile was mirrored back at her.

She tried it again. She ran a few steps away and charged
back screaming in rage at the disobedient mirror. Again a
beautiful and shining smile beamed back at her. She jumped
up and down again. She jumped up and down and up and
down and up and down. Could she possibly be imagining
that the image was actually *laughing* now? In fact it seemed
the angrier she got, the more the mirror laughed! In a total
rage, the Princess yanked off the queen's lovely gown and
ran from the room.

Later that night, the Princess sat alone in her room. The chambermaid had just turned down the beautiful snow-white coverlet of her little bed and had left her with a steaming cup of chocolate and some tea crumpets.

Anastasia wandered around her room. She sipped on the chocolate and nibbled on the crumpets. She wandered out on the balcony and could hear the soft strains of a singer not far off in the quiet night. He was probably singing his love ballad to one of the maidens who attended the Queen. She heard his gentle voice crooning his love song in the early evening.

> I sing my song to a lovely maid,
>   With soft and golden hair.
> She brings great joy into my heart
>   With her loving, gentle air.

The balladeer continued his song as Anastasia wandered back inside. Her mind was on other things. She wandered casually over to her mirror and seated herself before it. She looked at herself as reflected from the depths of the mirror. She could see the details of the beautiful white bedroom behind her. She could see her own small face encircled by a ring of golden curls. She could see her wide blue eyes looking back at her. She could see the lovely red gown she wore.

All of a sudden, she scowled at the mirror. The mirror scowled back. She scowled again into the mirror. Again the mirror scowled back. She took her hands and pushed her nose into horrible contortions this way and that way. The nose in the mirror likewise moved to this side and that side. Then she used her fingers to push her mouth into equally horrible contortions. The mirror image always did exactly the same.

How was it, then, that earlier in the day that *other* mirror had only smiled back at her?

Anastasia stopped for a moment and just studied the mirror quietly. This was a great puzzlement to her. She thought long and hard about this great mystery.

Suddenly Anastasia had an idea. She looked into the mirror and tried to smile. Oh, that felt funny! And it looked pretty strange, too. The mirror image didn't look like the one that she had seen in the mirror behind the King's meeting room. It looked more like her scowl.

Still experimenting, Anastasia took one finger and pushed up the corner of her mouth as she had seen it in the strange mirror. That was something like it. So she took another finger and pushed up the other corner of her mouth. That, too, was sort of like it. She studied her image for a moment. Then she let go her fingers. The mouth in the mirror fell down all of a sudden into its usual droop.

Confused and tired, the Princess crawled into her bed and drifted off into a deep sleep.

The next morning, Anastasia was so preoccupied that she forgot to grumble at the chambermaid. The chambermaid was puzzled by this but said nothing and quietly tiptoed away at her first opportunity. The chambermaid's exit was so quiet that none of the downstairs servants had their usual warning of the awakening of the little Princess.

Anastasia continued in this state of deep thought on down the stairs, stopping a moment in a halfhearted attempt to put on a proper scowl before proceeding to the kitchen. In the kitchen, she simply slipped quietly into her place at the table and hardly noticed as the cook put her bowl in front of her.

Puzzled, the kitchen maids and cooks looked quickly from one to another and shrugged their shoulders, not knowing what to make of this quiet little Princess. Anastasia then slipped quietly back through the front door of the kitchen and on out to the great hall, leaving the kitchen maids in the garden to poke their heads in, just a few moments later—having missed their usual cue to return to the kitchen when Anastasia slammed her way out the back door.

Lady Lillian showed very little surprise at the early morning visit by the Princess, and it took only a moment to let her in.

The Queen Mother seemed not at all surprised by the early visit, smiling as she greeted Anastasia.

"Good day, my child. How are you?"

The Princess quickly perched herself on the small stool and leaned over to rest her small elbows on the arm of the chair in which her grandmother was seated. She then rested her chin in her hands and looked up at the Queen Mother.

"I am most puzzled," she said thoughtfully.

"And how is that, my dear Princess?"

"I found a very strange mirror yesterday."

"And what do you feel was strange about this mirror?"

"It didn't work right, Queen Mother."

"How do you mean that this mirror did not work right, my child?"

"Well, when I looked in the mirror, at first it looked like a usual kind of mirror; but it wasn't quite like a mirror is supposed to be."

"Child, you must tell me more. I'm afraid I do not understand how this mirror was strange to you."

The Queen Mother was looking quite seriously at Anastasia. Anastasia thought for a moment that this was one of the few times that she had not seen her grandmother smiling. But, as the good lady continued to look seriously at her, Anastasia began again.

"It was a strange mirror because the picture in the mirror looked like me—except it *didn't* look like me!"

Anastasia stopped for a moment. She knew this had not made the confusion clear. Then she began again.

"You see, Queen Mother, in that mirror, I looked the same. The dress I was wearing was the dress I had on. It looked just the same. When I moved my arm, the mirror moved its arm—like so." And Anastasia slowly moved her arm to demonstrate. "Then when I would move my body, it would move the same way. The room in the mirror was the same as the room actually was. Everything in the mirror was the same as it actually was—except for my face. My face looked really strange! It was completely different from mine—like this." At that, Anastasia tried to get her face to smile the way she remembered it from the mirror.

Seeing the strange contortions of the Princess' small face as she tried to imitate the sweet smile of the mirror image, the Queen Mother began to laugh. She laughed hard, although she tried not to, for she could see that Anastasia was most serious about this matter. After the Queen Mother had laughed for a bit, she hid a big smile behind her hand and looked at the little girl from merry blue eyes.

"I'm sorry, dear. You *did* look most comical just then."

"But Queen Mother, that was what the girl in the mirror did to me! When I would do like this"—and Anastasia made a horrible scowl—"the mirror would do like this." Anastasia once again sent the Queen Mother into gales of laughter as she watched the little girl trying to imitate a most unfamiliar smile.

After the Queen Mother had once again brought herself under control, she looked quite thoughtfully into the face of the little girl. For a few moments she just looked quietly at Anastasia and thought deeply.

"I have heard talk of such a mirror," she finally said quietly.

"What *kind* of talk have you heard about this strange mirror?" Anastasia asked.

"It sounds to me as though you have discovered the Magic Mirror which shows to people their Higher Self."

"What is this Higher Self?" asked Anastasia.

"The beautiful smile you saw in the mirror is the *very best* of you. The mirror was reflecting back the *very best* that you can be. The *very best* that you can be is called your *Higher Self.*"

"Do you mean that what I saw in the mirror was actually *me?*"

"Yes, my dear. *It was you.* But it was not the person that you show the world every day. Instead, it was showing you what you *can* be *if you wish to be it.* It was showing you the *deepest* you, the *real* you, the happy little girl you were born to be."

"How is it I have not heard of this Higher Self before?" asked Anastasia.

"My child, my child: I have tried to tell you, but you were not listening."

The Queen Mother and Anastasia continued their chat at great length. Anastasia asked more questions, and the Queen Mother did her best to answer them all. They talked and talked and talked.

Finally, Lady Lillian announced the arrival of some other visitors to the Queen Mother. The Queen Mother apologized to the little girl and explained that she would have to excuse herself to go and greet her guests.

A nastasia busied herself as best she could. She visited the stables but had little to say. The stable boys were most puzzled by her quietness and stood and stared as she wandered up the stable path.

She visited the village as usual although, of course, much later than expected. Still deep in thought, she just strolled quietly between the thatched huts and nodded at an occasional villager. The villagers, too, were most puzzled by the strange behavior of the usually noisy and grumpy little Princess. Leaving the village, she made her usual trip through the garden.

The time dragged as Anastasia watched the sundial while the sun crossed the sky to the time when she felt that it would be all right to go to the little room behind the King's meeting room. At last the sundial threw its shadow at the right time, and she left the garden.

She crossed the great hall and went down the long hall to the King's room. It was empty, just as she had expected. Without wasting another moment, she crossed the office to the little door and entered the small room. In the doorway, she paused and looked across to the strange mirror. she approached it slowly, almost shyly; and as she came nearer, she leaned forward to peek into it. There again was the Princess with the sweet smile on her face!

She reached up to touch her own face and to feel the lines in it. They felt quite serious. The mirror, however, was still smiling gently. It continued to imitate her every move, just as it had done the day before, except for the facial expressions.

Anastasia drew closer. She very seriously studied the mirror. She walked to and fro in front of it again, quietly studying this person who was so new to her, this Higher Self of hers. Then she did a strange thing.

She sort of tiptoed behind the mirror and checked to see if there was something different about its back. The back just looked black all over and was held up by a few wood pieces surrounded by the same pretty golden frame that one could see from the front. She tiptoed quietly back to the front of the mirror and peeked into it again. The sweet little-girl face smiled out at her. Then she returned to the back of the mirror. There was no change. She began to walk to the front of the mirror again, but this time she tripped over something on the floor by the side of the mirror.

Anastasia was too late to catch herself. She fell sprawling full length in front of the mirror. And she hurt herself. She felt a pain in her ankle.

Anastasia started to cry. She curled herself up in front of the mirror and pulled her tiny ankle out from under her dainty gown to get a closer look. There on her ankle was a small but definite bruise. Yes, she had hurt herself, and here was the evidence. She grasped her ankle in both hands and sobbed in front of the mirror. She sat there for a few minutes, lost in the pain of her bruised ankle.

After a moment she glanced up,
and there in the mirror sat a little girl
in the same position as she was, holding
onto one ankle. But the mirror girl
was not crying. Instead she was
sitting there holding an ankle
and smiling brightly back
at the Princess.

For a moment, Anastasia was so astounded that she forgot to cry. She stared blankly into the face of the little girl in the mirror. Then she raised her tiny ankle and held it up to the mirror. She turned it to the mirror so that the Princess in the mirror could see the bruise there. The mirror image continued to smile angel-like back at Anastasia. But something else amazed Anastasia still more!

On the dainty little ankle of the girl in the mirror there was no bruise! Anastasia stared hard at the ankle in the mirror. She turned the ankle every which way, trying to reflect the small bruise in the mirror image, but it was no use.

Finally she pulled the ankle back to herself and looked it over very, very carefully. Yes, there on the tiny ankle near the shin bone was a small but definite bruise. She held it close to her for a moment and studied the bruise again and again. It was real. It was right there on her ankle.

She turned the ankle back to the mirror to see the mirror image of the small bruise. But none could be found. She turned her ankle every which way, but no bruise could be found in the mirror! And there sat that stupid little girl smiling out at Anastasia!

Anastasia sat there very quietly for a moment and then she began to cry again. She sobbed quietly for a few minutes and then studied the mirror face very closely. The only reaction she could get from it was that silly smile!

So Anastasia began to cry more loudly. She bent her head over her bruised ankle and sobbed very sadly while she peeked out from under her lashes to get the reaction of the girl in the mirror. Although the girl in the mirror repeated every other move that Anastasia made, the girl continued to smile broadly. Seeing this, Anastasia began to sob a little more loudly. The sounds she made were the saddest and most heartbroken she could get out. And still the mirror smiled brightly out at Anastasia.

Making the most noise she could, Anastasia began to howl directly into the mirror, holding her ankle up for the image to see. She howled and howled and howled, still watching the mirror-Princess for her reaction. However, the only reaction she could see was for the face to smile back still more brightly. Shocked by this, Anastasia was finally quiet for a moment.

Suddenly she could hear music. Anastasia held her breath and listened closely. The sound was coming from the mirror! She leaned toward the mirror and listened closely. The mirror was singing now!

Leaning closer, Anastasia could hear the words.

I sing my song to a lovely maid,
With soft and golden hair.
She brings great joy into my heart
With her loving, gentle air.

The mirror was singing the song of the balladeer that Anastasia had heard just outside her window the night before. She sat very, very quietly and listened as the words and the song continued. Finally, Anastasia stood up and quietly crossed the room. She walked through the little door and thoughtfully pulled it shut behind her.

Anastasia was very quiet the next day when she visited the Queen Mother. She laid her head in her grandmother's lap and turned to look up at the lovely lady as she spoke.

"The mirror behaved quite oddly yesterday, Queen Mother."

The Queen Mother began to stroke the soft golden curls of the little Princess.

"In what way do you mean the mirror behaved oddly, my child?"

"I hurt myself, Queen Mother." At this Anastasia sat up and uncovered her ankle, stretching it out toward the Queen Mother so that she could see the little bruise on it.

"Yes, it would appear that you did," commented the Queen Mother.

"Well, I did that yesterday when I was looking at the mirror. And when I fell, it wouldn't cry. And I couldn't see the bruise in the mirror. It just didn't seem to be there."

"Oh, I see." The Queen Mother was quiet for a moment.

"Why did it act like that, Queen Mother?" asked Anastasia.

"Well," said the Queen Mother, speaking slowly and thoughtfully, "I have never seen a Magic Mirror, so I would have to guess at the why of it all." She paused for a moment and then continued. "You must realize that the mirror would not cry when you cried because it feels no pain. That is to say, your *Higher Self* feels no pain."

The Queen Mother paused for a moment and then said, "Let me start at the very beginning. You see, inside of you lives a person who looks just like you and who moves just exactly the way you do. Only, this person was never born and will never die—never gets hurt, never feels sick, and is never unhappy or sad or any of those things that so many people experience while they are here on earth."

The Queen Mother thought again for a moment and then continued, "This person inside of you is called by some the *Higher Self* or the *God-Self*. It is *you*, but it is the *very best* of you. It is *God-as-you*, right here and right now. Since God never gets sick or feels pain and all of that, then of course your God-Self never does either."

Anastasia said quietly, "So that is why it would not cry when I hurt my ankle."

"Yes, child, that's right! It did not feel that pain as you did. It was *your* experience and not one that your God-Self would have."

"But why was she singing when I was quiet for a while?"

"It is said that when you are in the middle of your deepest hurts and angers and problems, your God-Self still knows only goodness and perfection. That is all your God-Self knows. And it is reflected in great joy and love. The most *glorious* feelings of all are the *only* feelings your God-Self has at any moment in your entire life. But you have to be quiet for a while and sort of turn inside yourself to hear your God-Self's joy and love. It is next to impossible to communicate with it when you are being very noisy or when you have your attention on other things."

"Queen Mother," asked Anastasia, "do I have a Higher Self or a God-Self because I am a *Princess?*"

"No, my child. *Every* human being on the face of the earth has a God-Self. Every slave and every King and Queen and all people in between have a God-Self."

"Surely you don't mean that the *chambermaid* has a God-Self, Queen Mother!"

"Yes, my child, she most certainly *does!*"

"Well then, you can't mean that the *cook* has a God-Self!"

"Yes, my child, she most certainly *does!*"

"Well, what about the *stable boys*? And the *villagers*?"

"They, too, have a God-Self. It belongs to every member of the human race!"

Anastasia sat and thought for a bit, puzzled by this piece of information. Then she asked, "Queen Mother, what is the mirror trying to tell me in showing me my God-Self?"

"Maybe it wants to show you how wonderful your life can be if you just allow your God-Self to work for you."

"You mean my God-Self will work for me?"

"Yes, my child. Your God-Self will help you to have all of the best that Life can offer if you will just listen and pay attention."

"Will it bring me *friends*, Queen Mother?" Anastasia asked.

"If you will listen and pay attention. You must leave now and think very carefully about what your God-Self might be trying to tell you."

Anastasia started the next day according to her old habits. The chambermaid once again brought her the wrong dress. Anastasia turned and barked at the poor woman, pointing out her error and ordering that she bring the correct dress immediately. But there was something different about the way she did it.

"You have the wrong dress again!" she barked. "Bring me the blue satin one!—Please."

The chambermaid did not believe her ears. The Princess had said "please." She had barked in her usual way—and then she had gently added "please." How very, very odd!

So the chambermaid brought the blue satin dress and quietly left the room.

Anastasia donned the lovely blue gown and started down the stairs. She was trying to return to her old ways and so she put her head down, grumbled and muttered and stomped. But something was wrong here. The rhythm was not quite right. She went stomp, mutter, grumble, *skip*. *Skip*, stomp, mutter, grumble. *Skip*, *skip*, stomp. This was a strange rhythm! She stopped at the mirror in the great hall and tried to fix a terrible scowl on her face, but the corners of her mouth turned up just a little bit in almost a grin.

Skip, stomp, mutter, grumble. Into the kitchen she went.

How strange Anastasia felt today!

The cook quickly put her bowl of oatmeal in front of her and left just as quickly, but not before she thought she heard Anastasia mutter a "thank you." Surely, she thought, she must have heard wrong!

The Princess ate quickly and ran out the back door of the kitchen. Skip, mutter, grumble, stomp. Skip, mutter, grumble, stomp. Skip, skip. Anastasia made her way to the stables. The kitchen cat saw her coming from his perch on the stable windowsill and just stretched himself sleepily in the morning sunlight. The kitchen dog got all prepared to run, but as he stood he noticed something different in the behavior of the Princess and just sat back down quietly to watch her approach.

The stable boys had seen her coming and busied themselves with their work. As they did so, they watched curiously. There was something quite peculiar about the little Princess today. As Anastasia walked away down the stable path, she was thinking: "Those stable boys have a God-Self, too!"

Anastasia continued on her way to the village. As she met the villagers one at a time on her stroll through the village, she was very careful to look very, very closely at them. One young mother was comforting her baby. Anastasia looked closely and lovingly and smiled a warm smile down into the child's face.

"Yes," Anastasia said to herself, "she has a God-Self. *I can see it!*"

As she walked on through the village, she saw a group of children playing ball. They seemed so filled with joy and happiness that it bubbled up from deep within them. They tossed the ball back and forth and chased one another and laughed and laughed and laughed.

"Yes," said Anastasia; "they have a Higher Self. *I can see it and I can hear it!*"

That day it seemed that everywhere Anastasia went she could see in other people some evidence of the beautiful God-Self that she now knew lived in her.

Somehow, as she continued her day's adventures, she found it most difficult to be grumpy. She kept thinking about that smiling, laughing, singing girl who lived inside herself.

Skip, stomp, skip, skip, stomp. Grumble, mutter, *giggle*. *Giggle, giggle*, skip, skip, *hop*. The rhythm changed more and more as the day went on and the heart of Anastasia grew lighter and lighter. Suddenly, she began running. She just ran for joy, with the wind in her face and the sun bright on her head. She ran until she was out of breath and then threw herself down beside the lovely flower garden that the gardener was planting.

As she lay there, she listened to the gardener as he whistled a little song, while he went about his planting. He kept his hands busy with his flowers and pots, and he whistled a joy-filled, happy song as he put the tiny plants into the warm, wet soil.

Anastasia lay quietly nearby, listening and watching. She knew she was seeing the Higher Self of the gardener as he worked. Yes, even the gardener had a God-Self!

After a few minutes of rest, Anastasia got to her feet again and quietly walked back to the castle.

She turned from the great hall into the long hall leading to the Queen's rooms. She walked proudly with her little head held high and a small smile, thinking about the beautiful God-Self she had been seeing.

As she neared the Queen's door, she spoke to the lady who stood there. "I wish to see the Queen," she said politely.

The Queen's lady paused to look closely at the Princess. She had changed somehow! What was different? She remembered the busy schedule of the Queen today and remembered some of the Princess' terrible tantrums in the past. But she looked so different today! Why, she was even smiling! The lady nodded and went back into the Queen's chamber.

A moment later, she reappeared. "The Queen will see you now."

Anastasia was so delighted to be allowed to visit the Queen that she smiled even more widely. She approached the Queen and curtsied politely before taking her place at the foot of the Queen's chair.

The Queen was looking strangely at Anastasia. In fact, all the ladies in the room were looking rather strangely at Anastasia. Whatever was the matter with them? Anastasia wondered. She turned and smiled brightly at each one.

Unable to resist the beautiful smile of the little Princess, each lady smiled brightly back at Anastasia. And the Queen smiled most brightly and most lovingly of all. What a pleasure to see her beautiful child so happy today!

And so the Queen and her ladies and the Princess had a most charming visit for the rest of the afternoon.

L ater that evening, alone in her room, the Princess was most surprised to receive a message from the King. She was wanted in the huge dining hall for the evening meal! This was a tremendous honor for one so young, and Anastasia was extremely pleased as she raced down the stairs.

At the bottom of the stairs, she stopped to check her reflection in the great hall mirror. She stopped for just a moment and a thought came to her. Deliberately, she allowed her little face to relax into the sweet and angel-like smile, just exactly as she had seen on the face of the girl in the Magic Mirror. Then she hurried on to the great dining hall.

The King's servant bowed as he opened the door to the great dining hall for the little Princess. Anastasia's heart was beating fast in her excitement at this oh-so-special invitation from the King.

Her eyes opened wide at the rich beauty of the great dining hall this night. Countless white candles lit up the great hall. The tables were piled high with the best food from all parts of the kingdom, and all the dishes were nicely displayed. The gold dinner plates and cups with the King's royal crest on them were set at the long banquet table, waiting for the dining guests.

The hall was filled with many beautifully dressed guests. The ladies wore very fine gowns of satins, laces, and velvets of every color imaginable. The King's men, his lords, his favorite friends, noblemen from all over the kingdom, and even some from nearby kingdoms, moved from group to group in their less colorful but just as good-looking uniforms. This had to be a very special occasion!

Looking quickly around the beautiful hall, Anastasia could see her parents, the King and the Queen, standing near the long banquet table visiting with some friends. The Queen saw her as the little Princess went over to her parents. She held out her arm to Anastasia and slipped it around the little girl's waist.

Anastasia stood quietly by as the Queen caught the attention of the King. He turned and looked down at the little girl. He was smiling warmly at his daughter, and Anastasia quickly curtsied out of respect for his being the King.

"Allow me to introduce you to my daughter, the Princess Anastasia," the King's voice seemed to boom throughout the large room.

The couple he had been speaking to turned toward Anastasia. They were a nice-looking couple, and they smiled kindly at her.

"Princess Anastasia, this is the good Lord Swanborough and Lady Swanborough."

Anastasia nodded her head very politely toward the beautiful lady and her handsome husband, just as a Princess should do.

"I am so pleased to meet you," she said shyly.

"And we are most honored to meet Your Highness," said the handsome lord. "May I introduce to you our daughter, Lydia. Lydia, this is Her Royal Highness, the Princess Anastasia."

Just then, a young girl exactly Anastasia's age stepped from behind the lord and lady and smiled sweetly at Anastasia.

"I am so pleased to make your acquaintance, Lydia," said the Princess.

The child Lydia was beautiful. She had long black hair and large brown eyes with sweeping dark lashes. Her skin was very clear, her cheeks were rosy and red. And she was just the same age as Anastasia! Could it be that Anastasia had met someone who could be her friend?

"Today is Lydia's birthday," said the King. "That is why your mother and I have given this wonderful party. I am pleased that you two can finally meet. Lydia has been quite lonely in her far-off corner of the kingdom, but now that Lord Swanborough's work for me has brought him and his family to live in the castle, I hope that you and Lydia will be able to get to know each other."

Oh, it was true! It was true! Anastasia could hardly believe her ears. Lydia had come to live in the castle! How glorious! She would have a friend of her same age living right here in the castle with her!

Anastasia smiled brightly at Lydia. Her heart was beating wildly now. She had never felt quite so wonderful ever before in her life. She could feel the brilliance of her smile and she knew that it matched exactly the beautiful smile she had seen in the Magic Mirror.

All the guests were soon seated at the great banquet table. Lydia was allowed to sit right beside Anastasia, and they whispered to each other as they ate the delicious food that had been laid before them. Anastasia was very careful to remember all her best manners.

After they had eaten, the big birthday party really began. The King and Queen had summoned all the best entertainers for this occasion.

First came the clowns. Oh how funny were the clowns!
They turned cartwheels right in front of Princess Anastasia
and Lydia. They had bright, funny faces painted on them
and they wore the long pointy shoes that all clowns wear.
Their clothes were too big and their hats were long. And
they performed acts of magic right in front of the two little
girls.

Anastasia looked at
Lydia, and Lydia was laughing. Anastasia threw her
head back and laughed too.
The clowns danced and
romped and tossed balls
high into the air. Then they
caught them. One caught his under his chin, and Anastasia and Lydia laughed at him. Then another one caught a
ball in his mouth, and Anastasia and Lydia laughed and
laughed. The girls looked at each other and then laughed
again. Oh, how glorious it was! Anastasia had a friend!

Then came the jugglers. They, too, had balls—many,
many balls, tossed high into the air and around and
around in circles. Anastasia
and Lydia laughed and gig-
gled some more. Anastasia
leaned over and whispered
to her new friend. Lydia
laughed again. Then
Anastasia laughed. What
great joy had filled the heart
of the little Princess!

Looking around the great banquet table, Anastasia saw the Queen watching them and smiling happily as she spoke to the King. She must have spoken of the little girls, because the King turned to look at them, too. Then he smiled broadly at them. Just then, Lord and Lady Swanborough turned to look at them, and Anastasia could see that they, too, were beaming at her and Lydia.

Anastasia turned in another direction and spotted the beautiful Queen Mother sitting just a little bit away. She excused herself for a moment and slipped over to speak to her grandmother.

"Queen Mother, I have a friend!" she grinned happily.

"So I see, my child. How very, very wonderful for you!"

"Did my Higher Self bring my friend to me, Queen Mother?"

"As I told you, my sweet Princess, when you listen to your Higher Self, it will help you to have the very best that life has to offer you."

"I think my Higher Self is very, very wonderful, Queen Mother!"

"That is most true, my child. You have changed so much since you first saw your God-Self in the magic mirror! Because you have changed and become like your God-Self, your brightness and joy are bringing to you friends who are also filled with brightness and joy, just like you. When you were angry and grumpy, you could not attract to yourself the friend you were looking for."

Anastasia was very quiet for a moment. She was thinking about what the Queen Mother had said.

"Queen Mother, when I was angry and grumpy, so was everybody else around me. Everybody except you, that is. Why were *you* never angry and grumpy with me, Queen Mother?"

"My child, my child, I always saw your Higher Self whenever I looked at you! When I saw the *very best* that is in you every time I looked at you, how could I possibly be angry and grumpy with you?"

Anastasia reached out and hugged her grandmother in a great bear hug. She planted a warm kiss on her beautiful cheek.

With her heart filled with great love and happiness, Anastasia fairly danced her way back to take her position beside Lydia again.

Here came the dancers. Anastasia and Lydia clapped their hands. Oh, how beautiful were the dancers! Oh, how joyful was the music! The dancers twirled and twirled, and Anastasia's happy heart danced and soared right along with the dancers.

Anastasia had learned her lesson from the Magic Mirror. She would never need to be angry or grumpy again, for she knew now how much joy and love and happiness were always deep within her, deep inside the beautiful God-Self, which would always be with her wherever she was.

This is a story—but it is also the truth. It tells you something wonderful about YOU. The part about the Higher Self, the God-Self, is really very, very true.

Inside each one of us lives a wonderful person that is our Higher Self. It is living there *right now*. In fact, *now* is an excellent, wonderful time to learn more about your very own God-Self! You can start with the person who gave you this book or who shared the story with you.

When you learn about your God-Self, when you turn to your Higher Self, you can have the same experience Princess Anastasia did. Everything will be brighter, happier, better!

Try it and you'll see!